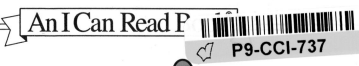

P9-CCI-737

Questions

Poems selected by

LEE BENNETT HOPKINS

Illustrated by

CAROLYN CROLL

A Charlotte Zolotow Book

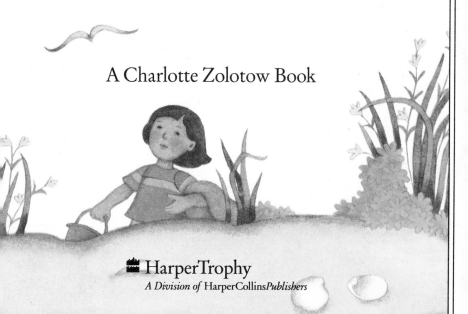

HarperTrophy

A Division of HarperCollins*Publishers*

Questions
Text copyright © 1992 by Lee Bennett Hopkins
Illustrations copyright © 1992 by Carolyn Croll
Printed in the U.S.A. All rights reserved.

Library of Congress Cataloging-in-Publication Data
 Questions : poems / selected by Lee Bennett Hopkins ; illustrated by Carolyn Croll.
   p.   cm.—(An I can read book)
 "A Charlotte Zolotow book."
 Includes index.
 Summary: A collection of poems that ask questions, by authors such as Aileen Fisher,
Lee Bennett Hopkins, Eve Merriam, and Ogden Nash.
 ISBN 0-06-022412-6. — ISBN 0-06-022413-4 (lib. bdg.)
 ISBN 0-06-444181-4 (pbk.)
 1. Questions and answers—Juvenile poetry. 2. Children's poetry, American.
[1. Questions and answers—Poetry. 2. American poetry—Collections.] I. Hopkins,
Lee Bennett. II. Croll, Carolyn, ill.
III. Series.
PS595.Q47Q47   1992   90-21745
811.008'09282—dc20   CIP
                                                                             AC

First Harper Trophy edition, 1994.

Acknowledgments

Every effort has been made to trace the ownership of all copyrighted material
and to secure the necessary permissions to reprint these selections. In the
event of any question arising as to the use of any material, the editor and the
publisher, while expressing regret for any inadvertent error, will be happy to
make the necessary correction in future printings. Thanks are due to the
following for permission to reprint the copyrighted materials listed below:

Curtis Brown, Ltd., for "Nighttime" by Lee Bennett Hopkins. Copyright ©
1974 by Lee Bennett Hopkins; "Philip" by Lee Bennett Hopkins. Copyright ©
1970 by Lee Bennett Hopkins. Reprinted by permission of Curtis Brown, Ltd.

Lillian M. Fisher for "Where Does the Field Mouse Hide?" and "My Favorite
Friend." Used by permission of the author, who controls all rights.

Harcourt Brace Jovanovich, Inc., for excerpt #12 from *Opposites* by Richard
Wilbur. Copyright © 1973 by Richard Wilbur. Reprinted by permission of
Harcourt Brace Jovanovich, Inc.

HarperCollins Publishers for a nine-line excerpt from "Square as a House"

To my great-niece
   Danielle Marie Yavorski
   Born February 27, 1988—
   Who is asking questions.
                        LBH

Who?

WHO AM I?

Felice Holman

The trees ask me,

And the sky,

And the sea asks me

Who am I?

The grass asks me,

And the sand,

And the rocks ask me

Who I am.

The wind tells me

At nightfall,

And the rain tells me

Someone small.

Someone small

Someone small

But a piece

of

it

all.

THE SECRET SONG

Margaret Wise Brown

Who saw the petals

   drop from the rose?

I, said the spider,

But nobody knows.

Who saw the sunset

   flash on a bird?

I, said the fish,

But nobody heard.

Who saw the fog

come over the sea?

I, said the sea pigeon,

Only me.

Who saw the first

green light of the sun?

I, said the night owl,

The only one.

Who saw the moss

creep over the stone?

I, said the gray fox,

All alone.

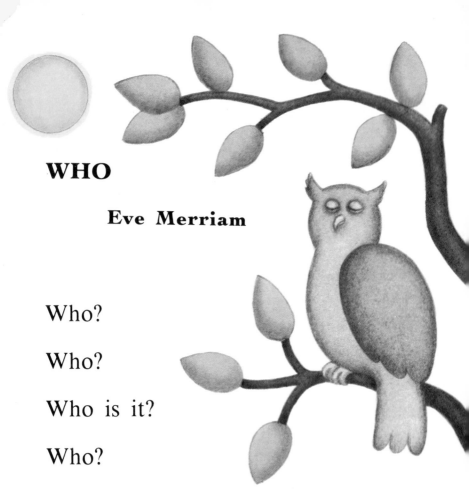

WHO

Eve Merriam

Who?

Who?

Who is it?

Who?

Isn't it you

who sleeps in the day

and wakes up at night

to go prying around?

Who?

12

Who?

Who is it?

Who?

Isn't it you

who has feathers so quiet in flight

that wings go flapping

as silent as clapping

without any sound?

Who?

Who?

Who is it?

Who?

        Isn't it you?

WHO HAS SEEN THE WIND?

Christina G. Rossetti

Who has seen the wind?
  Neither I nor you:
But when the leaves hang trembling,
  The wind is passing through.

Who has seen the wind?
  Neither you nor I:
But when the leaves bow down their heads
  The wind is passing by.

What?

from
SQUARE AS A HOUSE

Karla Kuskin

If you could be small

Would you be a mouse

Or a mouse's child

Or a mouse's house

Or a mouse's house's

Front door key?

Who would you

Which would you

What would you be?

WHAT DO I MAKE?

Ilo Orleans

People make

    All sorts of things,

Candy, or clothes,

    Or books, or rings;

Shoes, or socks,

    Or kettles, or pans,

Shovels, or rakes,

    Or watering cans;

18

Bread, or pie,

Or birthday cake.

But do you know

What I can make?

I can't make chairs,

Or toys, or dishes,

Or bats, or balls—

But I make WISHES!

19

from
WHAT IS PINK?

Christina G. Rossetti

What is pink? a rose is pink

By the fountain's brink...

What is blue? the sky is blue

Where the clouds float through.

What is white? a swan is white

Sailing in the light.

What is yellow? pears are yellow,

Rich and ripe and mellow.

What is green? the grass is green

With small flowers between...

What is orange? why, an orange,

Just an orange!

21

ANSWERS

Aileen Fisher

What weighs the littlest

you can think?

What hardly weighs at all?

"An aspen leaf," says Jennifer,

"that flickers down in fall."

22

"A milkweed seed," says Christopher.

"A thistledown," says Clive.

"A butterfly," says Mary Ann,

"and it's alive ... *alive.*"

from
OPPOSITES

Richard Wilbur

What is the opposite of *two*?

A lonely me, a lonely you.

Where?

AUGUST AFTERNOON

Marion Edey

Where shall we go?

    What shall we play?

What shall we do

    On a hot summer day?

We'll sit in a swing.

    Go low. Go high.

And drink lemonade

    Till the glass is dry.

One straw for you,

One straw for me,

In the cool green shade

Of the walnut tree.

WHISKY FRISKY

Anonymous

Whisky, frisky,

Hippity-hop

Up he goes

To the treetop!

Whirly, twirly.

Round and round,

Down he scampers

To the ground.

Furly, curly,

What a tail!

Tall as a feather,

Broad as a sail!

Where is his supper?

In the shell.

Snappity, crackity,

Out it fell.

WHERE DOES
THE FIELD MOUSE HIDE?

Lillian M. Fisher

Where does the field mouse hide?

Here in the meadow green and wide.

What is she weaving

Deep in the grass?

A snug little nest,

A soft round mass.

The tight little house

With downy floor

Will nestle her babies

Seven or more.

The tiny mice will grow and hide

Here in the meadow green and wide.

WHERE DO STARS GO?

Jean Conder Soule

Where do stars go when they sleep?

To fluffy clouds so snuggly-deep?

Are they very gently tucked in tight

By Mother Moon who says,

"Good night;

Sleep, my children, close your eyes

And the wind will croon you

lullabies."

FLYING-MAN

Mother Goose

Flying-man, Flying-man
Up in the sky,
Where are you going to,
Flying so high?

Over the mountains
And over the sea,
Flying-man, Flying-man
Can't you take me?

NIGHTMARE

Judith Viorst

Beautiful beautiful Beverly

Has asked me to a dance.

And I am dressed

In all my best:

My purple shirt,

My buckskin vest,

My cowboy boots,

My—oops!

Where are my pants?

When?

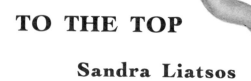

TO THE TOP

Sandra Liatsos

We're climbing and climbing
The trail is so high
that I think we'll be climbing
right up to the sky.
I want it to end
and my poor feet to stop.
Oh, when will we reach
the mountaintop?

36

TELL ME

Bobbi Katz

When does a pumpkin wear a smile?

When does a witch do a dance?

When does a skeleton rattle its bones?

The night when the goblins prance!

LOST

Sandra Liatsos

My dog has been gone

for a week and a day.

I miss his big bark

and the games we would play.

38

I am searching the streets

where he liked to roam.

Oh, when will he find me

and follow me home?

MY FAVORITE FRIEND

Lillian M. Fisher

When will we meet again

My favorite friend?

You've moved away.

You couldn't stay.

The yard is empty.

Your swing is gone.

Your chair is missing

From the lawn.

I wish you hadn't moved away

My favorite friend

Who couldn't stay.

BEING SOMEONE ELSE

Sandra Liatsos

When can I be someone else

instead of only me?

I'd like to be an astronaut

or a chimpanzee.

I'd like to be a racing car,

a monster, or a queen.

I guess I'll have to wait

until it's time for Halloween.

How?

SNEEZES

Valerie Osborne

How on earth

Do you suppose

A tickle gets into

And right up your nose?

HOW MUCH WOOD?

Mother Goose

How much wood

Would a woodchuck chuck

If a woodchuck could chuck wood?

A woodchuck would chuck

All the wood he could chuck,

If a woodchuck could chuck wood.

LIKE A SUMMER BIRD

Aileen Fisher

How would it be

to fly and fly

like a summer bird

in the rain-washed sky

after the sun

had ironed it dry?

How would it be

to sleep in a tree

on a rocking-chair branch

when the wind blew free,

with a sound in your ears

like the sound of the sea?

How would it *be*?

47

I AM

Dorothy Aldis

I am a bridge

From one bed to another;

I am a whale

With frightened fish to chase;

I am a boat

Sailing round my mother—

How can I be a little boy

And wash my hands and face?

HOW FAR?

Leland B. Jacobs

How far is a dream?
As far as a star
High in the sky?

How far is a dream?
At the close of the day
A dream is just
A pillow away.

NIGHTTIME

Lee Bennett Hopkins

How do dreams know

    just when to creep

Into my head

    when I fall off to sleep?

Why?

TELL ME

Dorothy Aldis

Tell me the reason I must wear

My rubbers in the rain.

I know I know.

But I don't care.

I like to hear again.

And *why* do I have to go to bed?

And *why* can't children fly?

Or tell me, for a change, instead:

WHY

Do I ask Why?

TWO FEET, FOUR FEET

Ilo Orleans

I have only two small feet,

But horses, dogs, and cows

Have four.

56

I can walk and run with

Mine.

So why do *they* need any

More?

PHILIP

Lee Bennett Hopkins

Why is it that

when I'm angry

at Philip

my whole day seems bad?

And why is it so

when we've settled our fight

my whole day just seems

to go perfectly right?

WHY

Prince Redcloud

We zoomed

to the moon

in just

a few years.

Why can't

we grow

onions

and

leave

out

the tears?

61

Index of Authors and Titles